NINJA

FIRST MISSION

CHRIS BRADFORD

With illustrations by
Sonia Leong

Barrington Stoke

For Stella, a little fighter

All proceeds from the sale of this book are
being donated to help fight her cancer battle

www.forstella.org

For more information on Chris and his books visit:

www.chrisbradford.co.uk

First published in 2011 in Great Britain by
Barrington Stoke Ltd
18 Walker Street, Edinburgh, EH3 7LP

www.barringtonstoke.co.uk

Reprinted 2014, 2015, 2018, 2019

Text © 2011 Chris Bradford
Illustrations © 2011 Sonia Leong

The moral right of Chris Bradford and Sonia Leong to be
identified as the author and illustrator of this work has been
asserted in accordance with the Copyright, Designs and
Patents Act, 1988

A CIP catalogue record for this book is available
from the British Library upon request

ISBN: 978-1-84299-939-4

Printed in China by Leo

Contents

Chapter 1
Floor-boards

Japan, Year 1580

I wait under the floor-boards.

I've been hidden here for over an hour, lying still as a stone.

My name is Taka. This is my first mission as a ninja and I must not fail.

I hear a door slide open and look through the crack in the floor-boards. I watch as a man crosses the room; his feet pass close to my face. He wears a gold silk robe with the crest of a black eagle on his back. He carries two samurai swords on his hip. Across his right cheek is a long red scar.

It's Lord Oda – the samurai warrior I've been waiting for.

The war-lord doesn't know I'm here. He can't see me under the floor. He sits down on his bed. In his hand, he holds a scroll of paper. He begins to read it.

"I never dreamed such things were possible," he mutters to himself.

After a few minutes, he puts the scroll into a wooden box by his pillow. He lays his swords beside his bed, blows out the candle and goes to sleep.

Outside, a full moon has risen over the castle. Its pale light shines through a small window and onto the cruel face of Lord Oda. Lord Oda is the sworn enemy of the ninja. My task is to stop him destroying our clan.

Now is the time.

I push softly at the loose floor-board above me and climb out of my hiding place. Using my ninja stealth skills, I cross the room without a sound. In the darkness I'm almost invisible. My black clothes and my hood turn me into a shadow. Only my eyes show.

As I draw close to the samurai lord, I see my hands are shaking.

Can I really do this? I ask myself.

I've been training to be a spy and an assassin all my life. But I'm still only fourteen. Have I learnt all the skills I need for this mission? Perhaps I *should* have waited for Cho. Can I save our ninja clan all on my own?

I have to prove myself. Tonight.

I'm now so close to Lord Oda, I can hear him breathe. As I reach out, my arm blocks the moonlight shining onto his face.

A small but fatal mistake.

Lord Oda's eyes snap open. For a moment, we stare at each other in shock.

Then he screams, "GUARDS!"

Chapter 2
Dragon's Gate

The Day Before ...

Holding the silver *shuriken* in my right hand, I take aim and flick the throwing star at the target. It flashes through the air like a mini bolt of lightning.

I've been practising with this weapon every day, but even I can't believe it when the *shuriken* strikes the tree trunk dead centre.

"Very impressive," says Sensei Shima as he walks over to me in the forest. "That's five out of five."

I bow to my teacher and kneel back in line with the other ninja students in the forest. A girl with long black hair smiles at me – Cho. She's a year older than me, and her acrobatic skills are the best in the clan.

"Well done, you *even* beat Renzo!" she whispers, looking over at a large sixteen-year-old boy with strong arms and a shaven head.

Renzo is glaring at me. He never comes second and he doesn't like it.

"It doesn't count," he grunts.

"Why not?" I protest.

"You're not a real ninja. You haven't gone on a mission yet."

Renzo loves to tell me this fact, and all my joy at mastering the Five Blades *shuriken* throw vanishes.

"You're just jealous," says Cho.

"Taka was lucky, that's all," snorts Renzo. "The *real* test is if he can do it under the pressure of a mission."

Sensei Shima claps for attention. "Time for unarmed combat practice," he calls. "Find a partner."

I look to Cho, but Renzo's already at my side, towering over me.

"I pick *you*," he snarls.

Before I can react, he grabs me by both arms. I try to shake off his grip, but he's too strong. Renzo throws me to the ground. I fight to get back up, but he drops on top of me and pins my arm down with his knee. I groan in pain as he presses with all his weight.

"Just as I thought," he grins and twists my arm so that the pain is almost too much to bear. "You wouldn't survive long in a real fight."

I'm forced to submit. I tap the floor.

"Change opponents!" orders Sensei Shima.

As I get up, I rub my hurt arm. It throbs.

Cho comes over to partner me. "Are you alright?" she asks.

I nod. "He's too strong for me," I answer.

My arm's fine – it's my pride that's been hurt. I'll never gain the respect of the others until I've completed my first mission.

"Everyone has a weak point," replies Cho. "I may be small, but few can beat me."

Without warning, she drives her thumb into the space behind my collarbone. A blinding pain shoots through my body, my legs go weak, and I fall to the ground.

"That's the Dragon's Gate," she smiles. "It's a pressure point that will take down the biggest and *ugliest* foe."

"Will you show me again?" I ask.

Cho repeats the move. Then she lets me try it on her. I press down and she collapses like a rag doll.

"Sorry, was that too hard?" I ask as I offer my hand to help her up.

"No, it was perfect," she replies. Then she grabs my wrist and, with a quick twist, throws me onto my back. "But that's the last time I'll let you win so easily."

"Stop training!" commands Sensei Shima.

Our clan leader, Tenshin, is walking towards us from the direction of the village. He's wearing his black *gi*, a ninja uniform with the crest of two hawks on the front. The two hawks are the emblem of the clan.

"We need all available ninja for an important mission," says Tenshin.

At last, here's my chance! I jump to my feet.

"Not you, Taka," Tenshin tells me. "This is a black-belt-only mission."

Chapter 3
Black Belt Test

"This will be my tenth mission," brags Renzo the next morning as the ninja team get ready to leave. "Tell me again, how many have you done, Taka?"

I ignore him and get on with filling everyone's water bottles from the village well.

"You haven't even passed the Grandmaster's black belt test!" Renzo sneers.

"Are you sure you can even do water duty on your own?"

My face goes red with shame as the other ninja try to hide their laughter.

The Grandmaster is the head of *ninjutsu*, the secret martial art of the ninja. When a student turns fourteen, the Grandmaster invites them to his temple to take a flower from his hand – without being detected. The Grandmaster must feel nothing, must not know they are even there. He is old and blind, but the task is far from easy. There are traps set all through the temple.

It's the ultimate test of stealth for a ninja.

Sensei Shima is the only ninja to have passed the test first time and that was ten years ago. Once a ninja earns their black belt, they're ready to be sent on any mission.

I've failed twice already. Am I ever going to succeed and get my black belt?

As I hand out the water bottles, I watch as my fellow ninja complete their final equipment checks. How I wish I could go too! But Cho isn't among them. Then I spot her crossing the village square towards me.

"The Grandmaster has asked for you," she says.

I stare at Cho. "Me? But why?"

"Why do you think?" Cho replies, grinning.

"*Black belt test!*" I exclaim. "But I'm not ready for it."

Renzo overhears us and gives a cruel laugh. "Those who fail to prepare, must prepare to fail!"

"Don't listen to him," says Cho as we walk away. "I've seen you practising every day. You're ready."

We cross the paddy fields, enter the forest and follow a path up into the mountains. As we draw near to the temple, I get more and more nervous.

"What if I fail again?" I ask Cho.

"Don't worry. It took me two attempts," she replies.

"But this is my *third*!"

Cho stops and looks at me. "I'll tell you a secret. As strong and skilful as Renzo is, it took him *five* attempts to get his black belt – not the two he brags about."

This news makes me feel better. But I'm still worried about my chances.

We climb a long flight of stone steps that lead up to a huge wooden gate. Cho stops before the temple entrance.

"I'll meet you later in the village," she says.

"Aren't you going on the mission?" I ask.

Cho shakes her head.

"But I thought all the ninja were going?" I say.

"I've been chosen by the Grandmaster for a special task," she tells me before she heads back down the steps. As I pluck up the courage to enter the temple, she calls out, "Good luck! And watch out for that second step."

Chapter 4
Grandmaster

I pass through the gate and into the temple's court-yard. In front of me is a large open square of grey gravel. On the other side is the temple – a tall wooden pagoda with a spire that pokes out of the top like a spear. To my left there's a beautiful rock garden, with a mountain stream flowing through it and into a pond.

The place looks empty. But I know the Grandmaster is waiting for me inside the temple.

As I'm about to step onto the gravel, I quickly pull my foot back.

I almost forgot. I must be nervous. This was how I failed my first attempt. The gravel is there to test a ninja's stealth-walking skills. The Grandmaster heard me crunching across the court-yard before I even got close to the temple.

I take three deep breaths to calm myself and I start again. Just like Sensei Shima's lesson, I point my left foot and I place my toes down first. Bit by bit I step onto that foot, letting the side then the heel touch the ground. This way I make no sound.

Half-way across, I head for the garden.

I don't want to make the same mistake I made on my second attempt. As the Grandmaster is blind, his sense of smell, as well as his hearing, is more sensitive. Last time he smelt the rich fertile earth of the paddy fields on my feet. This was another lesson in how to be invisible – a ninja must remove or cover up any smells that might give him away.

I stand in the mountain stream to wash the dust off my feet. Beside me I see there's a juniper bush. I remember the Grandmaster likes to burn juniper wood in the temple, so I pull off some leaves and rub them on my body. The plant's woody smell hides all traces of my scent. Once my feet are dry, I stealth-walk across the rest of the court-yard.

So far, so good.

I enter the temple. Inside, the main hall is cool and dark. A polished wooden floor leads to steps and a platform where the shrine is. At the centre of the temple, a bronze Buddha glistens in the light of two candles.

In front of the shrine, on the platform, sits the Grandmaster.

He is cross-legged on a cushion and his hands rest in his lap. He is so still he could be a statue. His face is old and wrinkled with a long grey beard. His eyes look straight at me, but see nothing.

In the palm of his right hand is a blood-red flower.

I creep across the room and am almost at the shrine's steps, when I remember Cho's warning.

Watch out for that second step.

I look closely at the step. There's a row of pins sticking out of the wood. They weren't there the last time.

I climb onto the raised platform, jumping over the second step. In just a few more paces, I'll reach the Grandmaster.

I'm so focused on getting to him without making a sound that I almost don't see the second trap. But a glimmer of light, like a spiderweb caught in the morning sun, alerts me to the danger. A thin cotton thread stretches across the room at ankle height. On one end is a little bell.

I'm now glad for all Sensei Shima's training. In lessons he'd make us walk through the forest looking closely at everything we passed to spot any traps – rocks we could trip over at night, or bushes and trees in which the enemy might hide.

He'd tell us, "*It's not what you look at, but what you see.*"

I step over the thread with great care and approach the Grandmaster. I can almost touch the flower and the Grandmaster still hasn't moved.

I stop for a split second. I can't believe I'm about to earn my black belt. There *must* be another trap. But I can't see one.

Just as I reach for the flower, the Grandmaster grabs my hand and pain rockets through my body. My body freezes as he presses a nerve point in my wrist.

The Grandmaster turns to me.

"Never assume a man with no eyes cannot see."

Chapter 5

A Lesson From An Ant

"I'll never be a ninja," I say, and I hang my head low.

"Your life is an unknown road," replies the Grandmaster, as we walk along a stone path through the temple garden. "How can you be so sure?"

"But without my black belt, I can't go on a mission."

The Grandmaster turns his blind eyes upon me.

"A black belt is nothing more than a belt that goes around your waist," he says. "*Being* a black belt is a state of mind. When your mind is ready, then you'll be a black belt."

"But I've failed *three* times," I sigh.

"Failure is success if you learn from it."

"So what did I do wrong?" I ask. "I avoided all your traps."

The Grandmaster smiles. "That you did. But you made three mistakes."

"*Three!*" I blurt out.

"The first mistake was coming in through the door. A ninja must never do what his enemy expects. Come from a different direction – the window, the roof, from behind or below. When you came through the door, your sound shadow gave you away."

"My sound shadow?" I ask.

The Grandmaster points to the sun, then to my darkened outline upon the ground. "Like the sun makes a shadow of your body, so it is with sound. As you passed through the door, you blocked the noise of the mountain stream. For a moment, the sound of running water became softer and I knew you had come."

"You noticed *that*?" I say, amazed.

The Grandmaster nods. "Close your eyes. What do you hear?"

"I hear the stream trickling and birds singing."

"Do you hear your own heart-beat?" he asks.

"No."

"Do you hear the ant that is at your feet?"

"No," I reply. I look down and see an ant carrying a leaf across the path. "Grandmaster, how can you hear these things?"

"Taka, how can you *not*?"

I understand now the Grandmaster is teaching me an important lesson in how to look and listen. I must watch and listen to *everything* around me.

"Your second mistake was not to match your breathing to my breathing," the Grandmaster says.

I don't understand. "How would that make a difference?" I ask.

"I could sense you as you got closer. You need to be in harmony with your target," he explains. "Remember, for a ninja, a small error is as deadly as a big one. When you jump over a canyon it doesn't matter if you get half-way or miss by an inch, you still fall to your death."

The Grandmaster drops his blood-red flower into the stream.

As I watch it float away, he goes on, "Your third and final mistake was to let doubt enter your mind, to become unsure. At the last moment you stopped for a split second, didn't you?"

"Yes, Grandmaster," I admit, and I bow my head in shame. "But I just didn't think I could do it."

"Always believe in yourself," the Grandmaster says firmly.

"How can I, when I keep failing?"

"Take your lesson from the ant," replies the Grandmaster. He points to the insect still trying to drag the leaf across the stones. "Whatever the size of the task or the things in its way, the ant never gives up."

With a last tug, the ant pulls the leaf off the path and carries on with its journey through the grass.

"You see, Taka," says the Grandmaster, resting his hand on my arm. "It doesn't matter how slowly you go, so long as you don't stop."

Chapter 6
The Scrolls

"Grandmaster!" cries Cho, running through the gateway. "The Scrolls have been stolen!"

We both turn to her in shock. The Scrolls are the secret teachings of the ninja. Written upon them is everything the Grandmaster knows, and all that the Grandmasters before him knew – weapon skills, hand-to-hand fighting methods, the Seven Disguises, the

Sixteen Secret Fists, the Death Touch, deadly poisons and even ninja magic.

"What happened?" asks the Grandmaster.

"I visited the Hidden Shrine as you asked," replies Cho, out of breath, "but when I got there it had been attacked."

"What about Monk Osamu who was guarding it?" asks the Grandmaster. On his old face I see worry for his old friend.

"He's alive but badly beaten."

"Does he know who did this?"

Cho nods. "They were samurai. They wore the black eagle crest of Lord Oda's army."

The Grandmaster gives a deep sigh. "This comes as no surprise."

I clench my fists in anger at the news. For as long as I can remember, Lord Oda has been our enemy. While some samurai hire the ninja as spies and assassins, most do not trust us and a few, like Lord Oda, want to destroy us all. What makes it worse for me is that this samurai lord murdered my father during the Battle of Black Eagle thirteen years ago. Because of him, I never met my father.

"We must get back the Scrolls," the Grandmaster says, slamming his fist into his palm. "Lord Oda must not learn our secrets. If he does, our clan is doomed. He will defeat us. Tell me, when did the attack take place?"

"Early this morning," Cho replies.

"We still have time," the Grandmaster says. "Black Eagle Castle is a day's march from the Hidden Shrine, but a ninja can speed-run there in half the time. Send our two best ninja at once."

"All our ninja are on a mission," Cho tells him.

The Grandmaster strokes his grey beard, thinking hard. "Cho, you must go alone then. It'll be very dangerous, but – "

"I'll go with Cho," I say.

"This is *not* a test, Taka," replies the Grandmaster. "You could get killed."

"You told me that being a black belt is a state of mind. That I must believe in myself. Well, I can do this if you give me the chance."

"I know how you feel about Lord Oda," the Grandmaster says. "You want to fight him for what he did to your father. But you *cannot* allow the wish for revenge to take away your focus. That could lead to failure."

"I seek justice, not revenge," I reply. "To get back the Scrolls will be justice."

The Grandmaster stares at me. I know he can't see, but it feels like he's looking deep into my soul.

"So be it," he says with a grave look on his face. "Complete the mission and *nothing* else. The fate of our clan is now in your hands."

Chapter 7
Black Eagle Castle

I speed-run through the forest, moving like the wind between the trees. Cho is ahead of me. She leaps over a log, as light and fast as a young deer.

We carry almost nothing since we need to be fast. I have my *shuriken* stars in my pack. Cho has a grappling hook on her belt and a sword strapped to her back. We are both dressed head-to-toe in the black uniform of the ninja.

We climb high into the mountains and take a short-cut into the next valley. We must catch the samurai before they get to their castle.

Cho helps me across a rocky river-bed and up the other side. I'm panting now and my legs shake with the effort of the climb. As we get to the top of the ridge, Cho suddenly stops.

"We're too late," she gasps.

I look down into the gorge below where a fast-flowing river runs. Marching up the road, a troop of samurai cross the river's only bridge and enter Black Eagle Castle.

The castle rises out of the rock like the broken tooth of a giant. A high wall surrounds the castle on all sides. Samurai guards armed with spears and swords stand on the battlements.

"What do we do now?" I ask Cho.

"Wait here until sunset," she says. "Then enter the castle."

"Do you know where the Scrolls will be?"

"No," Cho replies. "But if we find Lord Oda, we find the Scrolls."

I try not to show my alarm at this plan. Back at the temple, I was confident. Now I've seen the castle, with its high walls and armed guards, I'm no longer so bold.

The sun drops behind the mountains and the gorge grows dark. In the night sky a full moon rises.

"Time to go," says Cho, running along the ridge to where a tall tree has fallen and now spans the gap.

"We'll cross one at a time. You go first," orders Cho.

I take a look at the tree she wants me to use as a bridge and an ice-cold shiver of fear runs down my spine. The river roars far below and I'm glad I can't see the terrifying drop in the darkness. As I cross, the tree creaks and groans like it's about to break.

"Keep going!" hisses Cho.

Once I get to the other side, Cho follows. She's more bold than me and gets across in a few easy leaps.

We now climb down the mountainside behind the castle. It's very dangerous. The cliff face is steep and it's hard to see where to put my hands and feet. But we can't risk being seen by the samurai.

At last we reach the bottom and I breathe a sigh of relief.

We hide behind a rock as a samurai patrol passes by, then we make a dash for the castle wall. Cho throws her grappling hook high into the air. It catches on the top of the wall and we climb up the rope.

Then we're inside the castle and we must stay alert. Samurai are everywhere. My heart is thumping in my chest as we creep down a flight of stone stairs and into a court-yard. In the centre is a water well, on the other side a storehouse and in the far corner a cherry-blossom tree.

As we make our way across the court-yard, we hear the sound of foot-steps. We duck inside the storehouse and watch four guards walk by.

"There are too many patrols," whispers Cho. "You stay here, while I find out where Lord Oda is."

I nod and Cho vanishes down a passage-way. I want to do more than just hide but I know Cho's acrobatic skills will allow her to

move through the castle without being seen. She'll find Lord Oda far quicker on her own.

As I wait for her to return, I hear voices coming from the opposite direction. Two men stride into the court-yard, with guards all round them. One is short and round as a ball. He's talking loudly to the other, who is tall and looks like a warrior. This man is dressed in a gold silk robe with a black eagle crest on his back. In the light of a lantern, I spot the red scar on his cheek. It's Lord Oda!

The war-lord Oda leaves the court-yard with his guards and I wonder what to do. *Should I follow? Or should I wait for Cho?*

If I wait, we might lose Lord Oda. If I go, I could find the Scrolls.

This is my chance to prove myself as a real ninja.

Chapter 8
A Difficult Choice

I stay hidden in the shadows as I follow Lord Oda to the castle's main tower. A short while later, I see lamps being lit on the third floor.

I tell myself I must remember the Grandmaster's lesson – I must enter the tower from a different direction. I climb the outside wall up to a third floor window. When I look in, I see a painting of a black eagle on the ceiling. This must be Lord Oda's bedroom.

His mattress is rolled out on the floor, ready for the night. Beside his pillow is a wooden box. A picture of two hawks is carved on the lid. Two hawks – the emblem of our clan. I've found the Scroll box!

I can hear Lord Oda and the other man talking in the next room. Without a sound I climb in through the open window. It's very narrow, but I'm small enough to slip through. When I climb down, I land on a loose floorboard. It squeaks as my feet touch it.

In the other room the voices stop.

I've a split-second to decide – I can climb back out the window ... or hide.

Lifting up the loose floor-board, I clamber into the hole below and lie down. Just as I lower the board back into place, the bedroom door slides open.

"There's no one here, my lord," says a guard, his sword at the ready. "It must have been a mouse."

"We can't be too careful now we have the Scrolls," says Lord Oda. "Double the number of patrols."

"We already have, my lord," answers the guard.

"Then double them again!" Lord Oda orders.

The guard bows and closes the door.

I decide to stay put. Now I know Lord Oda has the Scrolls, I only have to wait for him to go to bed. Then I can steal them as he sleeps. My only worry is Cho. She will think I've been caught.

By the time Lord Oda puts the Scrolls back in their box and settles down to sleep, my body is stiff from lying in the tiny space under the floor-boards. I climb softly out of my hiding place and creep across the room towards the sleeping samurai. I match my breathing to his breathing, just as the Grandmaster told me.

By the pale light of the moon, I can see Lord Oda's swords lying next to his bed. It would be justice for this samurai to die by his own sword.

In my head, I hear the Grandmaster say, "Complete the mission and *nothing* else."

I have to make a choice – the Scrolls or the sword …

As I reach out, my arm blocks the moon-light that shines onto Lord Oda's face.

A small but deadly mistake.

Lord Oda's eyes snap open. For a moment, we stare at each other in shock.

Then he screams, "GUARDS!"

I grab the Scroll box and make a dash for the window. But Lord Oda grabs me before I can get there. I fight to break free, but he's too strong. As Lord Oda reaches for his sword to kill me, I thrust my thumb into the nerve point behind his collarbone.

The Dragon's Gate.

He cries out in pain and drops to the floor.

I stuff the box in my pack and scramble out the window as the guards rush into the room. They're too big to follow me through. I clamber down the tower as fast as I can. When I am back on the ground, I run to the court-yard to find Cho. But she's nowhere to be seen.

All of a sudden samurai guards appear from every direction and block any hope of escape.

Chapter 9
The River

"Kill him!" snarls the head guard.

The samurai draw their swords and attack. I take out my *shuriken*.

The pressure is on. Five throwing stars. Five samurai.

I can imagine Renzo's gloating face waiting for me to fail.

I throw one *shuriken* after the other. I hit the first samurai in the hand. He drops his sword. The second throwing star strikes the next man in the chest. The third catches the head guard in the throat. The fourth samurai is stopped by a *shuriken* star in his arm. The fifth *shuriken* ... misses.

It hits the cherry-blossom tree instead. The last guard swings his sword to cut my head off. It's too late for me to avoid the blade.

At the last second, Cho drops from the tree like a black butterfly. She knocks the guard aside with a flying front kick. The tip of his sword just misses my neck.

The guard attacks Cho. As he cuts down with his sword, Cho leaps forwards and grabs his arms. She spins into him, then throws him over her shoulder. He flies through the air and falls down the well. There's a terrified scream then a *splash!*

Cho turns to me. "I saw you climbing down the main tower. Did you get the Scrolls?"

I nod.

"Let's get out of here then!" she says, as more samurai pour into the court-yard.

We run up the stairs to the top of the wall. There are samurai everywhere now. A guard sees us and shouts for more men.

"Hold on to me," says Cho, and she throws her grappling hook around a stone statue sticking out of the battlements.

The samurai close in. Cho leaps from the wall. I hang on for dear life as we swing through the air. The ground comes rushing towards us. Cho lets go at the last second. We land, roll and jump to our feet.

Without stopping, we sprint for the bridge. There's no point climbing the cliff. We'd be shot down with arrows. Our only hope is to out-run the samurai.

But as we reach the river, we see the guards have raised the draw-bridge.

"We'll have to swim," says Cho. She looks scared as she stares at the fast-flowing waters.

"The Scrolls will be ruined," I say.

"What other choice do we have?" says Cho, as the gates to Black Eagle Castle open and a mass of samurai pour out.

We look for another point to cross the river. But there's nothing. Only a few trees and a grove of tall bamboo next to the river-bank.

All of a sudden I have an idea.

Chapter 10
Decoy

"Where are we going?" asks Cho as I lead her into the bamboo grove. The samurai are behind us and they are getting closer.

"Up!" I reply.

Cho gives me a puzzled look.

"Trust me," I say, and I clamber up the tallest bamboo stem.

As we both reach the top, the bamboo bends under our weight. It swings down and across the river, and we fly through the air until we're hanging over the opposite bank. We both let go and drop safely to the ground.

The bamboo straightens up again as the samurai appear on the other river-bank. They stare at us in shock.

"How did they get *across*?" shouts one of the samurai.

"They must have flown!" cries another.

"It's ninja magic," says Lord Oda. We see him walk between them with his gold robe glimmering in the moonlight.

As we vanish into the darkness, he bellows, "Ninja, be warned, I'll have my revenge!"

Everyone from our village is at the temple to see us return the Scrolls.

With Cho at my side, I climb the long flight of stone steps.

"I hear you failed your black belt test … *again*," says Renzo, as we pass him on the stairs.

"An ant never gives up," I reply. "*You* of all ninja should know that after *five* attempts."

It takes Renzo a minute to work out what I mean but then his face goes red. His friends turn to him and it's clear they can't believe what they have just heard.

As Renzo tries to explain away his lie, Cho and I cross the court-yard to the temple. The Grandmaster is standing outside. We kneel before him and I hand over the Scrolls.

He takes the precious box from me and puts a black belt in my hands in its place.

"But I didn't pass your test," I say.

"The Scrolls were the test," he answers with a smile. "And you passed."

"But what if I'd failed?" I say. "Lord Oda would have all our secrets."

"I knew you wouldn't fail," the Grandmaster tells me. "This time you *believed* you'd pass. That is sometimes all it takes."

The Grandmaster laughs. "Anyway, they weren't the real Scrolls."

I stare at him in shock. "We risked our lives for fake Scrolls?"

The Grandmaster shakes his head. "Your mission was very important. I knew Lord Oda wanted the Scrolls. So I let him find them. However, I replaced the real ones with fakes."

"So why send us to get them back?" I ask.

"If we didn't try to steal them back, Lord Oda would guess they were fake," he explains, and I start to understand his cunning plan. "Now he thinks he knows our secrets. He thinks what he read in the Scrolls is true!"

The Grandmaster begins to laugh. "Lord Oda will think ninja can pass through walls like a ghost, transform into spiders, and even fly like a bird!"

Cho and I look at each other, and laugh.

"But *we* did!"

The End

Our books are tested
for children and young people by
children and young people.

Thanks to everyone who consulted on
a manuscript for their time and effort in
helping us to make our books better
for our readers.

Join Taka on his next mission ...

Ninja: Death Touch

Taka is now a black belt and is learning the lethal arts of the ninja. He will need these skills to protect his clan. Lord Oda has sworn to destroy all ninja.

As Oda's samurai army marches on their village, Taka must fight once more, and this time his whole world is at stake ...

Ninja: Assassin

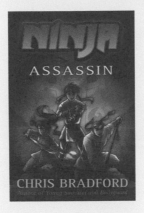

With his ninja clan on the run and his mother dead, Taka vows to find Lord Oda and bring him to justice.

But Taka's training is not yet complete. Can he fulfill his destiny as an assassin?

Or will a dark secret prevent him from completing his deadly mission?

www.barringtonstoke.co.uk